Some words about vampires:

"Be afraid. Be very afraid."
Jack Beechwhistle

"I'm coming to get you!"
A vampire bat

"WoooOoOoOo."
A haunted tea towel

"Has anyone seen my broom?"
A forgetful witch

"Has anyone seen my head?"
A headless ghost

"Gulp!"
Daisy

More Daisy adventures!

DAISY AND THE TROUBLE WITH LIFE

DAISY AND THE TROUBLE WITH ZOOS

DAISY AND THE TROUBLE WITH GIANTS

DAISY AND THE TROUBLE WITH KITTENS

DAISY AND THE TROUBLE WITH CHRISTMAS

DAISY AND THE TROUBLE WITH MAGGOTS

DAISY AND THE TROUBLE WITH COCONUTS

DAISY AND THE TROUBLE WITH BURGLARS

DAISY AND THE TROUBLE WITH SPORTS DAY

DAISY AND THE TROUBLE WITH PIGGY BANKS

Published for World Book Day 2016:
DAISY AND THE TROUBLE WITH JACK

Also by Kes Gray:

JACK BEECHWHISTLE:
ATTACK OF THE GIANT SLUGS

DAISY

and the TROUBLE with
VAMPIRES

by Kes Gray

RED FOX

RED FOX

UK | USA | Canada | Ireland | Australia
India | New Zealand | South Africa

Red Fox is part of the Penguin Random House group of companies whose addresses
can be found at global.penguinrandomhouse.com.

www.penguin.co.uk
www.puffin.co.uk
www.ladybird.co.uk

First published 2016

001

Set in VAG Rounded Light 15pt/23pt
Printed in Great Britain by Clays Ltd, St Ives plc

A CIP catalogue record for this book is available from the British Library.

ISBN: 978-1-782-95608-2

Penguin Random House is committed to a sustainable future
for our business, our readers and our planet. This book is
made from Forest Stewardship Council® certified paper.

To the Adams Family

CHAPTER 1

The **trouble with vampires** is people shouldn't be allowed to dress up as them.

Or talk about them. Or even think about them. Especially at Halloween. Vampires can be really scary at Halloween. So can all the other Halloween scary things. Not that anything scares me or anything.

It's just that when people like Jack Beechwhistle keep talking about scary things at school ALL THE TIME, including vampires, then after a while, things can get a bit scary-ish.

Nothing scares me most of the time, at least not during the daytime anyway. Vampires don't scare me in the daytime, zombies don't scare me in the daytime or ghosts or werewolves or even the hooley-hooley man. They did scare me a little bit on actual Halloween night, but that was different, because Halloween night is the scariest night in the world, especially if you go trick-or-treating for the first time with an actual vampire, who isn't an actual vampire, but you think she is, because she told you she is, but then she tells you she isn't, but by then you've already decided she is, because grown-ups aren't meant to tell fibs or even say the word vampire, especially if you haven't been trick-or- treating before. WHICH ISN'T MY FAULT!

CHAPTER 2

Did you know *Halloween* is short for '*Hallo, we know* something you don't know'? I didn't either. Jack Beechwhistle told me as soon as I walked into school with Gabby last Monday.

The **trouble with someone telling you that they know something you don't know** is it makes you want to know what it is.

Even if it's Jack Beechwhistle doing the telling. Trouble is, I'd forgotten it was the beginning of Halloween week.

The **trouble with Halloween week** is I didn't know that there was even such a thing as Halloween week.

I thought there was just Halloween *night*. But Jack said he wasn't waiting until Saturday for Halloween to begin. As far as he was concerned, we should start getting afraid on Monday.

Not just afraid either. *Very* afraid.

When me and Gabby told him we weren't afraid of anything, Jack said he knew things that were so scary they would make the blood freeze in our veins.

Plus, if we didn't believe him, then we should ask Colin and Harry.

The **trouble with Colin and Harry** is they are Jack Beechwhistle's best friends, so they agree with everything he says. Even if the things Jack says are a bunch of whopping fibs.

Me and Gabby told all three of them

that we absolutely totally weren't
listening to anything they had to say
about Halloween week, and that if
they kept saying things that were
scary, we would tell Mrs Peters. Mrs
Peters is our teacher and she can be
proper scary.

Trouble is, instead of saying more scary things to us, Jack said them to other people instead.

"Hallo, we know something you don't know!" he said, getting everyone to gather around him in the playground and then making evil slurping noises with his mouth.

The **trouble with Jack making evil slurping noises** is that it makes you want to hear what he is going to say next. So we had to listen. Especially as it was a story about a haunted drinking fountain.

According to Jack, the drinking fountain in our playground gets its water from the wicked well.

The **trouble with the wicked well** is it's full of wicked frogs and wicked newts, which means if you drink from it at midnight on Halloween night when there's a full moon, you'll be chased by werewolves.

Me and Gabby told everyone that everything Jack was saying was a lie. But Jack said, if we'd never drunk

from our school fountain at midnight on Halloween night when there was a full moon, how could we be sure?

Which was kind of true and really annoying, because we couldn't prove he was fibbing.

Jack said the only way to defend yourself against werewolves is to shoot them with a gun that fires silver bullets. Or a crossbow that fires silver crossbow bolts. Or a massive castle catapult that fires silver boulders. Werewolves are allergic to silver.

There were other scary things he said too.

"Did you know that if you hang your

coat up on a certain coat hook in the classroom at midnight on Halloween night when there is a full moon, then the ghost of an evil headmaster from ten centuries ago will float down the corridor wearing your coat and going 'WOOOOOOOO!'?"

Me and Gabby told everyone that there were no such things as haunted coat hooks or haunted headmasters, but Jack said, if we'd never hung up a coat in school at midnight on Halloween night when there was a full moon, how could we be sure?

Which was kind of true again, and even more annoying this time –

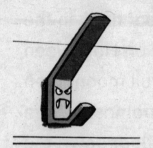

because do you know what he said next? He said that the most haunted coat hook in our classroom was the one I hang my coat on!

And the second most haunted was Gabby's!

And he didn't stop there either.

He told us that pencil cases can be haunted,

pencil sharpeners can be haunted,

 rubbers can
be haunted,

even bendy rulers
can be haunted.
What a load of fibs!

Trouble is, Colin and Harry totally backed him up, so some people in our class thought it was true. Paula Potts wouldn't even open her pencil case when we sat down for lessons in case a haunted compass tried to stab her.

And it didn't stop there either.

15

Jack didn't stop telling scary stories on Monday, Tuesday, Wednesday, Thursday or even Friday. He kept telling us things we didn't know and didn't even want to know ALL WEEK!

CHAPTER 3

When I met my mum after school on Monday, I told her all about Jack.

"Daisy," she said, "Jack and his friends are just trying to give you the heebie-jeebies. There are no such things as werewolves, werefoxes, werechickens or wereanythings."

"What about werepuddles?" I asked. "Jack says, if you tread in a puddle at midnight on Halloween night when there's a full moon, you'll turn into a weregoldfish."

"There are no such things as weregoldfish either," said my mum. "You shouldn't believe a single word Jack Beechwhistle says."

As soon as I was totally sure that Jack had been telling lies all day, I felt much better.

I felt even happier when Mum told me that my nanny and grampy would

be coming for Sunday lunch the day after Halloween! I love Sunday lunch, especially when we sit at the table and have a tablecloth and everything. It feels so special!

"Can we have a roast dinner?" I said.

"Yes," said my mum.

"Can we have crackling?" I asked.

"Yes," said my mum.

"Can we have roast potatoes?" I asked.

"Yes, we can have roast potatoes," said my mum.

"You forgot Yorkshire puddings," whispered Gabby.

"Can we have Yorkshire puddings?" I asked.

"Yes, we can have Yorkshire puddings," said my mum.

"Can we not have peas?" I asked.

"Yes, we can not have peas," sighed my mum.

"Or Brussels," I laughed.

"Definitely no Brussels," said my mum, smiling.

"But we can have gravy," I said.

"Yes, we can definitely have gravy," said my mum. "If you're extra good, I'll make a trifle too!"

Before I said goodbye to Gabby, we made a BFF pact never to listen to

Jack Beechwhistle again.

"Unless we can't help it," she said.

"Unless we have no choice," I said.

"Because he's talking too loud," said Gabby.

"Or we're standing too close," I said. "Apart from that we are absolutely totally not going to listen to one single word Jack Beechwhistle says ever again."

"Absolutely totally," said Gabby, opening her front gate and giving me a wave goodbye.

"Pinkie promise!" I said, giving

her a wiggle-wave back.

"PINKIE PROMISE!" she shouted, wiggling her little finger back at me and then closing her front door.

"PINKIE DOUBLE PROMISE!" I shouted, holding both my little fingers up and then remembering to tell my mum not to forget the apple sauce. I love apple sauce. Especially on roast dinners!

CHAPTER 4

The **trouble with pinkie double promises** is they are really hard to keep, especially during Halloween week.

You'll never guess what Jack Beechwhistle said to everyone in the playground on Tuesday. He said 666 is the devil's telephone number.

Which means if you play hopscotch in the school playground during Halloween week and you miss square six three times in a row, your head will explode.

It was a good job Gabby and me

had been listening, because if we hadn't, we wouldn't have been able to tell everyone that Jack was telling whopping fibs again.

"How do you know I'm fibbing?" said Jack.

"Because no one would ever play hopscotch in the school playground at midnight on Halloween night when there's a full moon!" I shouted.

"Did I say anything about midnight?" asked Jack.

"Noooooooo!" said Harry, shaking his head really slowly.

"Did I even mention a full moon?" asked Jack.

"Nooooooooo," said Colin, shaking his head even more slowly than Harry did.

"All I said was 'if you play hopscotch in the school playground during Halloween week'," said Jack, stroking his chin and then giving me the evils with his eyes.

The **trouble with Jack Beechwhistle giving you the evils with his eyes** is it makes you want to give him the evils back. Trouble is, before I had even got my eyebrows into the right position, he had started clapping his hands, stamping his foot and shouting, "DARE! DARE! DARE!"

The **trouble with someone shouting "DARE! DARE! DARE!" in the playground** is it makes everyone else shout it too. Even when they're meant to be on your side.

"If you're so sure that I'm fibbing," said Jack, "then you won't be afraid to play Halloween hopscotch in front of us right here, right now, will you?!" he laughed. "Stand back, everyone! You don't want to get

Daisy's brains all over you when her head explodes!"

It was no good. Everyone was looking at me now, even Gabby. Not only that. The "DARE! DARE! DARE!" shouts had got even louder.

Gabby told me I should take absolutely no notice of the "DARE DARE DARE!" shouts, but I absolutely had no choice. I was absolutely going to have to play Halloween hopscotch whether I wanted to or not. Even if my head ended up exploding. Even if my brains ended up going all over the playground. Luckily, I had a plan.

My plan was to spend so long throwing my stone from square number one to square number five, I wouldn't have time to even get to number six before the lunch bell went.

Unluckily, Jack had a plan too. He said I could start at square number six.

The **trouble with starting at square number six** is it means you're in the danger zone straight away. Because you haven't had a chance to practise your stone throwing.

Or rolling. Or anything.

So I thought of another plan. My second plan was to spend so long looking for a stone to throw that the bell would ring before I even had a chance to start playing.

Only Jack had a second plan too. He got Colin and Harry to get a stone for me.

When I said the stone they'd got me wasn't the right shape for rolling or throwing, the "DARE! DARE! DARE!" shouts changed to "CHICKEN! CHICKEN! CHICKEN!" shouts, so I had to start playing straight away.

The **trouble** **with** **playing** **straight away** is it's really hard to roll or throw a stone straight onto a number six hopscotch square. Especially if you're using a wrong-shaped stone, double especially if you haven't had any practices, and triple especially if the "CHICKEN! CHICKEN! CHICKEN!" shouts change to "MISS! MISS! MISS!" shouts.

"MISS! MISS! MISS!" shouts can really put you off.

So I missed.

I tried really hard, but I still missed.

As soon as my stone rolled past the number six square, everyone apart from Gabby started cheering! Which was so wrong. Because I would never want to see someone's head explode in the playground playing hopscotch. Not even Jack Beechwhistle's.

But they still kept doing it.

And doing it and doing it.

So I missed again.

Which meant I only had one throw left.

The **trouble with only having one throw left** is it makes you think you're definitely going to miss again, especially when the "MISS! MISS! MISS!" shouts changed to "EXPLODE! EXPLODE! EXPLODE!" shouts.

The more I heard "EXPLODE!", the smaller the number six square looked.

The smaller the number six square looked, the harder it got for me to aim.

The harder it got for me to aim, the surer I was that I was going to miss.

So I missed again – by quite a long way actually.

As soon as my stone bounced past

the number ten square, everyone around me jumped back and covered their ears. Apart from Gabby. Gabby knew all along that my head wasn't going to explode. So did I actually. Which is why I wasn't really bothered whether I missed or not.

"HAH!" I said to Jack Beechwhistle, pointing at my head with both of my

pointing fingers. "Who's the fibber now?"

But Jack just folded his arms. "I didn't say WHEN your head would explode" – he grinned – "I just said it would explode."

Honestly, that boy is the worst!

The **trouble with doing afternoon lessons thinking your head is about to explode** is it makes it really hard to concentrate. Was I pleased to hear the school bell ring at the end of the day!

When I met Mum outside the school gates, I asked her straight away if my head was actually going to explode.

"Daisy, I told you yesterday not to take any notice of Jack Beechwhistle," she said. "If he knows he can wind you up, then he will wind you up! So, just ignore him!"

So that's what me and Gabby definitely, absolutely, totally decided we would do. We wouldn't look at Jack Beechwhistle. We wouldn't go near Jack Beechwhistle. In fact, we would NEVER listen to Jack Beechwhistle EVER AGAIN!

QUADRUPLE PINKIE PROMISE!

CHAPTER 5

You'll never guess what Jack said to us on Wednesday. (Apart from "Hallo, we know something you don't know.")

He said there's a zombie graveyard buried under our classroom!

The **trouble with having a zombie graveyard under your classroom** is that if it's midnight on Halloween night when there's a full moon, the zombies can wake up!

Apparently when a load of zombies all wake up at the same time, it's called a zombie rising. But if they all wake up and decide to take over the world, it's called a zombie invasion!

Invasion

Gabby told Jack that he was the biggest liar in the world, because once you're dead you're dead, so you can't wake up, because to wake up you have to be able to open your eyes, and to be able to open your eyes you have to be alive, not dead.

But Jack said that's how zombies work. Their deadness is so alive, they can rise up out of their graves, dig themselves out of the ground with their long creepy fingernails, and then hold their arms out and come and get you!

When I asked Jack what zombies are made of, he said, "Evil gunge."

He said the gunge inside a zombie is so evil that bullets can't stop them, missiles can't stop them, even the SAS can't stop them.

"If you want to fight a zombie, then the only way to defeat them is to fight gunge with gunge," Jack said. "Especially at midnight on Halloween night when there's a full moon."

When I went back to my desk after break on Wednesday, the only thing I could think about was the zombie under my feet.

Gabby told me there weren't any zombies under my feet. She said

I shouldn't be listening to a word Jack Beechwhistle says.

Trouble is, it definitely felt like there was a zombie underneath me. Especially when I opened my desk lid.

The **trouble with desk lids** is that mine creaks. I'm sure it never used to creak, but it definitely creaked on Halloween Wednesday.

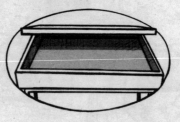

When I told Jack Beechwhistle about the creak at lunch time, he said it might not have been my desk lid that I'd heard creaking. He said it might have been the evil rusty hinges of a zombie coffin lid opening right beneath my feet! Not during Halloween night, during maths!

The **trouble with the lid of a zombie coffin** is once it's open the zombie can climb out.

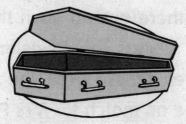

The **trouble with zombies climbing out** is it could be the start of a zombie rising or invasion.

When I told Gabby that a zombie rising or invasion was about to start right underneath my desk, she said I was being silly. She said, first there are no such things as zombies, second there are no such things as zombie risings or invasions, and third, even if there were, the zombies would be no match for Mrs Peters.

Trouble is, Gabby hadn't noticed my school socks.

The **trouble with my school socks** is I always pull them right up in the morning when I put them on.

Only when I looked down at my socks after lunch, they weren't pulled up at all. Both of them were pulled right down!

It was almost as if a zombie had reached through the classroom floor during lessons and used his creepy fingernails to pull my socks down when I wasn't looking!

I sat cross-legged on my chair after that – well, until Mrs Peters told me to sit properly. Even then I didn't put my feet on the floor. I'm telling you, if there was going to be a zombie invasion in our classroom on Wednesday afternoon, there was no way I was going to be the first one to get grabbed!

When I told Mum about my school socks, she said she was starting to think she was the only person on the planet who hadn't gone Halloween crazy.

"SCHOOL SOCKS?" she said. "A ZOMBIE HAS PULLED DOWN YOUR SCHOOL SOCKS?"

My mum doesn't believe in Halloween. I think that's why we

have never gone trick-or-treating together. Or carved a pumpkin. Or had a Halloween party at our house. The only Halloween party I've ever been to was at Vicky Carrow's house. Which is a good thing actually, because a Halloween party with my mum around would be no fun at all.

"I told you Jack Beechwhistle would wind you up if you let him," she said. "Hasn't he got any homework to do? Hasn't he got a football to kick around in the playground?"

"He prefers telling Halloween

stories," I told her.

"Well, I'd prefer it if you stopped listening to them," she said. "The next time Jack starts telling Halloween stories, promise me you will cover your ears."

"I promise," I fibbed.

CHAPTER 6

Did you know there are three main types of ghost?

Jack Beechwhistle told us about them during morning break time on Thursday. At first me and Gabby weren't going to listen, but we were standing quite close by, so we had to.

According to Jack, the three main types of ghost are:

1) Normal ones
2) Ugly ones
3) Headless ones

Headless

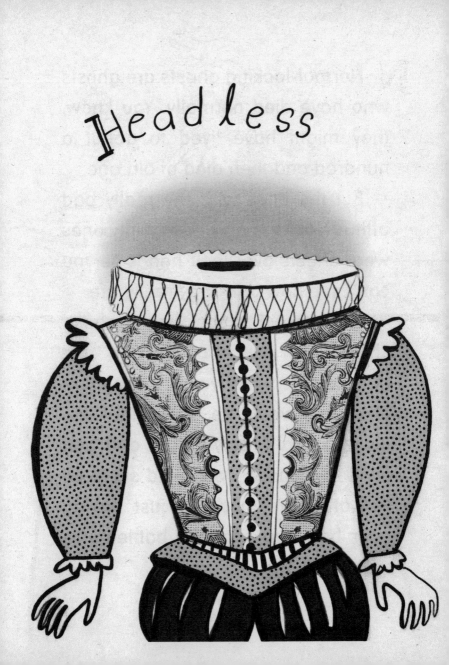

Normal-looking ghosts are ghosts who have died normally. You know, they might have lived to about a hundred and then died of old age.

But the ones with the really bad attitude are the ugly ones. Ugly ones wear sheets over their heads so you can't see how ugly they really are.

Gabby said if she was a ghost, she'd much rather be an ugly one because the uglier you are, the more scary you would be. She said if you were a really ugly ghost and you lived in a castle, you could scare all the attackers away by just poking your head up over the battlements and going "WOOOOOOO!"

But Jack said that isn't how ghosts with sheets over their heads work. They do go "WOOOOOOO!" but they also do much worse things than that. At first, me and Gabby didn't believe him, but when he started whispering, we knew it must be true.

Apparently, a ghost with a sheet over its head won't just chase after you going "WOOOOOO!" If it catches you and gets really close, it will suddenly lift its sheet up and show you how ugly it is underneath. If you look straight at it with frightened eyeballs, you TURN TO STONE!

The **trouble with being turned to stone** is you have to stand really still all the time.

And it makes you really heavy. Imagine going to the swimming baths after you've been turned to stone!

Or doing PE!

And that's not all you have to be afraid of during Halloween week either. According to Jack, it isn't just sheets with ghosts under them that you have to watch out for – it's ordinary sheets too! And blankets and bath towels and tea towels and T-shirts and flannels, and even socks!

Jack says, if you have a laundry basket in your house on Halloween night and it's piled up with things that haven't been ironed, they can turn into ghosts too! Especially at midnight on Halloween night when there's a full moon.

How scary is that?!!

When I asked Jack how to defend yourself against a haunted tea towel, he said you have to pin it to the clothes airer with silver clothes pegs.

Trouble is, my mum's clothes pegs are red, yellow, green and blue!

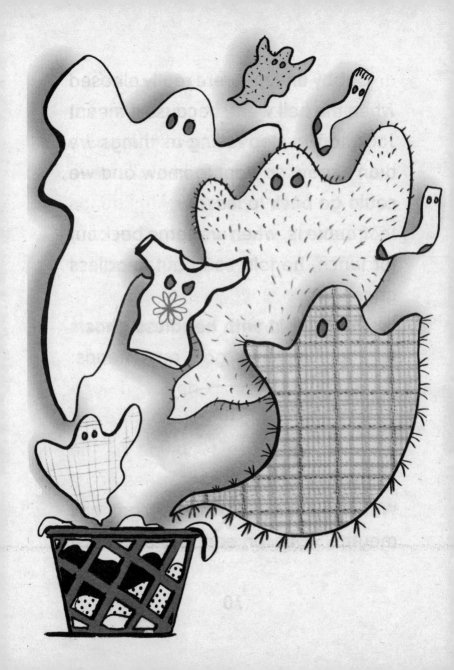

Gabby and me were really pleased when the bell went, because it meant Jack had to stop telling us things we didn't know or want to know and we could go back to lessons.

Trouble is, when we came back out for lunch, he told us about headless ghosts too.

The **trouble with headless ghosts** is they haven't got any heads.

Which means they haven't got any mouths, eyes or ears either. Which

means they can't go "WOOOOOO,"
they can't see where they are going,
and they can't hear how noisy they
are being when they bump into things
in the night.

Jack says the proper name for
headless ghosts is POULTRYGEISTS!
Or at least, I think that's what he said.

I wonder if headless ghosts can
get headaches?

CHAPTER 7

The next day Jack's stories got even scarier!

"Hallo, we know something you don't know!" Jack, Colin and Harry shouted the moment me and Gabby walked into the playground on

Halloween night eve morning. "Did you know all your mums could be witches in disguise?!"

"Our mums don't look anything like witches!" I told them. "Witches have warts and whiskers and long pointy noses!"

"Our mums don't have warts or whiskers or long pointy noses!!" said Gabby.

"Maybe not at the moment, they don't," Jack said, "but what about at midnight on Halloween night when there's a full moon?"

According to Jack, Harry and Colin, there are far more witches around than you'd ever realize. There are white witches and black witches and even sand witches. The trouble is, most of the time they are dressed in totally ordinary clothes.

The **trouble with totally ordinary clothes** is they make people look totally ordinary.

I wear ordinary clothes, Gabby wears them, you wear them – everyone wears them.

Trouble is, so do our mums!

The **trouble with mums who wear totally ordinary clothes** is, if they were actually real witches, you would never know! Especially if they can do spells on themselves that make their faces look ordinary too!

Jack Beechwhistle said that, in the olden days, mums who were witches were really easy to spot, because not only did they have warts and whiskers and pointy noses, they wore black clothes, black shoes, black stockings and black pointy hats. So, to stop themselves from being spotted, chased and captured,

they decided to become secret witches
instead! With secret broomsticks too!

According to Jack, every secret witch has a spell that can make her broomstick go undercover.

Before the spell, it would look like this:

But after the spell it could look like this:

this:

78

or even this:

According to Jack, the only way to defend yourself against a secret witch is to take away her magic wand. Trouble is, secret witches have spells that make their magic wands go undercover too.

Before the spell it would look like this:

But after the spell it could look like this:

this:

this:

or even this:

"You don't think your mum could be a secret witch, do you?" asked Gabby as we walked back to class after morning break.

"No way," I said.

"Has your mum got a broom in her cupboard?" she asked.

"Yes," I said.

"Mine too," gulped Gabby.

"Does your mum have a mop in her cupboard?" she asked.

"Yes," I said.

"Mine too," gulped Gabby.

"And a hoover," we both said together.

"And a pepper pot and a wooden spoon and a toothbrush and a razor," I whispered.

"A razor?" gasped Gabby.

"Not in the broom cupboard," I

said. "In the bathroom cupboard."

"Why would your mum need a razor?"

"To shave her legs, I think," I said.

"Not her face?" asked Gabby.

"I don't think so," I said.

"But it could be her face?"

"She hasn't got any whiskers," I said.

"Maybe she shaved them off!" gasped Gabby. "Are you totally sure your mum isn't a secret witch?"

"I'm not sure of anything any more," I said.

"Me neither," frowned Gabby. "Me neither!"

CHAPTER 8

When we went back to class after morning break on Friday, me and Gabby absolutely, totally definitely, one million thousand hundred per cent promised each other that we wouldn't listen to one single word more that Jack Beechwhistle said about Halloween for the entire total rest of the week.

Cross our hearts and hope to die.

Trouble is, I had strawberry jam sandwiches in my lunch box.

The **trouble with strawberry jam sandwiches** is they look like blood sandwiches. At least, Jack Beechwhistle says they do.

The **trouble with blood sand-wiches** is that's what vampires eat.

At least, Jack Beechwhistle says they do.

According to Jack, the only thing vampires eat is blood. They don't eat burgers or chicken nuggets or baked beans or even ice cream. Unless they're *blood* flavour.

Jack says vampires are a bloodthirsty cross between a ghost and a zombie. Except, instead of wearing sheets, they wear black capes, and instead of gunging you to death, they suck all your blood out with their evil teeth.

Plus – and this is the scariest bit – they can turn themselves into bats. Not cricket bats . . . the ones that fly around upside down in the sky at night!!!!

The **trouble with upside-down bats that fly around in the sky at night** is, if you leave your window open at midnight on Halloween night when there's a full moon, they can fly into your bedroom when you're sleeping and get you. I think they can even get you if you're awake!

Jack Beechwhistle says as soon as a vampire bat flies into your bedroom at night, it turns the right way up, magics into a proper-sized vampire and goes sniffing for blood. Especially if it's midnight on Halloween night when there's a full moon.

According to Jack, the only way to scare a vampire away is to put garlic all over  your bedroom. Trouble is, my mum doesn't like garlic. She says it's too smelly.

Gabby says her mum and dad absolutely love  garlic and that they are always putting it in their cooking at home. Which means that at midnight on

Halloween night when there's any type of moon, Gabby will be able to defend herself.

But what about me? The only thing I'd be able to do is close my bedroom windows and draw my curtains!

When I asked Jack if vampire bats could get into your house anywhere else apart from windows, he said no – apart from letter boxes, chimneys and cat flaps.

The only one of those I haven't got is a cat flap!

Gabby said she was sure I wasn't going to get my blood sucked out on Halloween night, and even if I did, all

I had to do was scream as loud as I could, and my mum would run into my bedroom and scare the vampire away.

"But what if my mum is a secret witch?" I said. "If my mum is a secret witch, she might be out on her undercover broomstick! She might be whizzing through the sky doing undercover cackles or looking for things to do undercover spells on! If she's whizzing around the sky on our broom or our mop or our hoover, she might not even hear me screaming for help! Our hoover is really noisy!"

"I hadn't thought of that," said Gabby.

"I have," I said. "I've thought of everything!!!"

Except I hadn't.

Because as soon as we'd put our lunch boxes away, Jack gave us the hooley-hooley man to think about as well!

CHAPTER 9

The **trouble with the hooley-hooley man** is I never really knew who he was.

I'd heard my friends talking about him at Vicky Carrow's Halloween party, but to be honest, I don't think anyone I know has ever really known who he truly is or where he truly comes from. Or what he truly looks like. Or what he truly does.

Jack Beechwhistle did, though.

According to Jack Beechwhistle, the hooley-hooley man isn't made out of sheets, gunge, bats or even meat. He's a skeleton made out of cobwebs. Or at least he's a skeleton with so many cobwebs on him, he looks like he's made out of cobwebs.

When Jack told everyone how the hooley-hooley man turned into a skeleton covered in cobwebs, he didn't even need to whisper, it was so scary.

Apparently about a thousand years ago, a farmer's boy called Fernando received an invitation to

a Halloween party. Fernando lived in a small village at the bottom of a mountain. On top of the mountain was a castle, and inside the castle lived the people who were having the party.

What Fernando didn't know was that he was the only person in the village who had been sent an invitation.

What he also didn't know was that the people in the castle who invited him weren't people at all – they were ghosts! (Not the ugly ones with sheets on their heads . . . The ones without sheets that look normal.)

When Fernando arrived at the party, everything seemed all right. There was lemonade and party hats and everything. But just before midnight, as the full moon began to rise, the ghosts asked Fernando if he wanted to play Halloween hide-and-seek.

Because Fernando was so little, he was really good at hide-and-seek, and so he was really keen to play.

"Run, Fernando! Hide, Fernando!" said the ghosts, covering their eyes and then turning to face the wall. "Hide in the very best place you can, and we will come looking for you when we've counted to a hundred."

Fernando ran to the west wing of the castle and found a small wardrobe in a child's nursery to hide in.

Once inside, he closed the door, hugged his knees, and waited.

And waited and waited and waited.

Days went past. Weeks went past. Months went past, and still no one came looking for Fernando.

Years went past, leap years went past, and still there was no sign of Fernando ever being found.

After about thirty-five years Fernando gave up hiding and tried to get out of the wardrobe. But he couldn't . . . because he wasn't a little

boy any more – he had grown up into a man!

"Why didn't the ghosts go looking for him?" Gabby asked.

"They did," said Jack, "but only once they'd finished doing all of their counting."

"They only had to count to a hundred!" I said.

"A hundred years," whispered Jack. "When ghosts play Halloween hide-and-seek, they don't count up to a hundred in ones, they count up to a hundred in years!"

"A HUNDRED IN YEARS!" everyone gasped.

"A hundred in years." Jack nodded. "A hundred years later, when the ghosts finally went looking for Fernando, ready or not, all they found in the wardrobe was the wedged-in skeleton of a grown man in a party hat covered in cobwebs!"

"FERNANDO!" gasped Gabby.

"Fernando," said Jack. "Fernando
had climbed into his hiding place a
boy, but had died in his hiding place
a man . . . a man that legend now
calls the hooley-hooley man – just a

party hat, cobwebs and bones."

It was the most blood-freezing story anyone in the playground had ever heard.

"Why did he change his name from Fernando to the hooley-hooley man?" I asked.

"He was adopted by owls," said Jack. "It was owls who went hoo-hoo that kept him alive all those years,

by flying into the nursery and feeding him field mice."

"URRRGGGH!" said Gabby. "Field mice?! I wouldn't eat a field mouse if I was the last owl on earth."

"You would if your life depended on it," said Jack.

"Why didn't the owls tell Fernando that the ghosts were counting up to a hundred in years?" asked Barry Morely.

"Why didn't the owls tell Fernando's mum and dad that

he was trapped in the castle?" asked Sanjay Lapore.

"Hoo-hoo knows?" whispered Jack. "The only thing I can tell you is that at midnight on Halloween night when the moon is full . . . the hooley-hooley man goes hunting."

"Hunting for what?" I gasped.

"A new wardrobe to hide in." Jack shivered.

The **trouble with new wardrobes to hide in** is the one in my bedroom is only three months old. Plus it's got really nice handles on the doors.

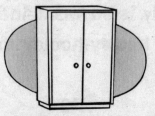

"What if he chose a nearly new one with really nice handles?" I said, not wanting to give too much away.

"The only way to stop the hooley-hooley man once he's inside your wardrobe is to grab his party hat, tear it into a hundred pieces and then get all the cobwebs off him with a feather duster," said Jack, as we walked back to class for afternoon lessons. "A feather duster made out of golden dodo feathers."

"But golden dodo feathers are extinct!" said Gabby.

"Exactly," said Jack. "And so will you be if the hooley-hooley man comes knocking tomorrow night. Especially if it's midnight, you're alone in your bedroom, the owls are hooting, the werewolves are howling, the zombies are gunging, the witches are cackling, the vampires are flapping, your mum is asleep, and there's a full moon."

CHAPTER 10

When I woke up on Saturday morning, all I wanted to do was stay in bed and hide under my covers. Because now it wasn't just Halloween week any more, it was actual Halloween night day!

Trouble is, Mum said I had to come downstairs for my breakfast.

"When does Halloween night day stop and Halloween night night actually start?" I asked her.

"It doesn't start at all in our house, Daisy," she said. "In our house,

October the thirty-first is just a day like any other day."

"But if we lived in someone else's house, what time in the day would Halloween night actually begin?"

"I haven't really thought about it," said Mum.

I had. I'd thought about it a lot.

"Say we lived in Jack Beechwhistle's house . . ." I said. "Would Halloween night start when it starts to get dark, or would it start when everything outside is well dark?"

"If we lived in Jack Beechwhistle's house, then it would probably be Halloween all day every day," said Mum.

"What if someone knocked on our door at nine o'clock in the morning and said, 'Trick-or-treat?' Would that mean Halloween day had finished and Halloween night had started?"

"No, Daisy, it wouldn't," said Mum. "Trick-or-treaters don't knock on doors on Halloween morning. Trick-or-treaters are only allowed to go trick-or-treating at night-time."

"Jack Beechwhistle says he never goes trick-or-treating," I said.

"You surprise me," said Mum.

"Jack Beechwhistle says he only goes trick-or-tricking."

"That doesn't surprise me," said Mum.

"Jack Beechwhistle says treats are for wimps."

"Does he now?" said Mum.

"You should hear some of the Halloween tricks Jack Beechwhistle says he's done on people," I said.

"I have a feeling I'm about to," sighed Mum.

"He's put a real alive python through someone's letter box," I said. "He's put soldier ants down someone's chimney . . .

and he's filled a post box with super-sucking quicksand. Once he even took the batteries out of a lighthouse, so the lights didn't work. Loads of ships crashed onto the rocks

because of his trick-or-tricking."

"I'm sure his mum and dad will be very pleased to hear that," said Mum.

"His mum and dad don't care," I told her. "Jack says he's allowed to do whatever he wants whenever he wants to do it. He says he can go out on his bike anywhere he wants, as late as he wants. Even when there's a full moon!"

"I doubt that very much," said Mum.

"It's true!" I told her. "It's true!"

CHAPTER 11

The **trouble with full moons** is I wasn't sure what time of day they started either, so as soon as I had finished my breakfast I went out into my back garden to get a good look at the sky.

"Hello, Daisy," said our neighbour Mrs Pike. "Are you trick-or-treating tonight?"

"We don't do Halloween," I told her.

"DON'T DO HALLOWEEN?" she

gasped. "I love Halloween! I adore Halloween! HOW CAN ANYONE NOT DO HALLOWEEN? When I was a girl, Halloween was my favourite night of the year! All those ghosties and ghoulies and long-leggity beasties  and things that go bump in the night! IT'S SO SCAAAAARY! IT'S SO FRIGHTENING!! IT'S SO EXCITING!! SURELY EVERYONE DOES HALLOWEEN?!"

"We don't," I said.

But she wasn't listening.

"Let's have a pumpkin off!" she said. "You carve yours, I'll carve mine and we'll get the nation to vote on whose is best!"

"We don't do pumpkins either," I told her.

"DON'T DO PUMPKINS?!" she gasped. "I love carving pumpkins!

I adore carving pumpkins! SURELY EVERYONE CARVES PUMPKINS ON HALLOWEEN?!"

The **trouble with saying you don't do Halloween or pumpkins to someone** is the someone you say it to should really understand you don't do Halloween or pumpkins. Especially if it's a grown-up someone.

But Mrs Pike didn't seem to understand at all.

"WHY DON'T YOU COME ROUND

FOR HALLOWEEN?" she said. "YOU COULD CARVE A PUMPKIN AND THEN WE COULD GO TRICK-OR-TREATING TOGETHER! You would love trick-or-treating, Daisy," Mrs Pike said. "It's so much FUN. Do you like sweets? If you like sweets, you'll LOVE trick-or-treating!"

It was just my luck. All I'd wanted to do was go back to bed and hide under my covers, but all Mrs Pike wanted to do was talk about carving pumpkins and trick-or-treating! Carve a pumpkin? I didn't want to go anywhere near a pumpkin!!! Especially after the things Jack

Beechwhistle told me when school ended on Friday:

Did you know, if the pumpkin you buy is haunted, the teeth you carve with your pumpkin carver can actually turn round and bite you? Jack told me.

Did you know that, on average, ninety-seven children get at least one finger bitten off by haunted

pumpkins each year? Fifty-three end up losing an arm! Jack told me.

Mrs Pike didn't seem to know half as much about pumpkins as Jack Beechwhistle.

Or Halloween sweets.

Did you know that Halloween sweets are poisonous? Jack says they are, so if you get any when you go trick-or-treating, whatever you do, don't eat them. Jack says you should give them all to him.

When I told Mrs Pike I didn't do pumpkins OR poison, she still didn't seem to understand what I was saying. It was almost like she had been put under a special Halloween spell herself!

"I know, Daisy! Why don't you and me have a special Halloween afternoon and evening together! Come round at four. I've got some

pumpkins that need carving and some fizzy blood that needs drinking, and then afterwards we can go trick-or-treating together too!"

FIZZY BLOOD? Things were getting serious now. I needed an escape plan and I needed one fast.

"I'll have to go and ask my mum," I said.

"Why don't you ask her now?" said Mrs Pike. "She's standing right behind you."

When I turned round and realized that Mum had come out to rake the lawn, I was so relieved. I was absolutely sure she would save me.

But she didn't!

"BRILLIANT IDEA, Veronica!" she said. "Daisy's been going on about Halloween all week! Of course she can go trick-or-treating with you tonight. Then I can make a trifle for Sunday lunch while she's gone."

"I'm going to take Daisy in my car to the best trick-or-treating road I know!" said Mrs Pike.

And then things got EVEN WORSE!

"Don't forget to dress up!" she said.

CHAPTER 12

Did you know that if you're still wearing a Halloween costume at midnight on Halloween night when there's a full moon, you will turn into the actual Halloween person you are pretending to be? Even if you've taken the costume off and it's on your bedroom floor, the bad magic can still happen.

Jack Beechwhistle told me.

There was no way I was going to get turned into a Halloween anything by dressing up in a costume for

Halloween. And anyway, I didn't have anything that I could dress up as.

"Put a sheet over your head and go as a ghost," said Mum, completely forgetting that I'd done that before.

"I wore a sheet to Vicky Carrow's," I told her. "And anyway, I'm bigger now."

"Cut two eye holes in the tablecloth instead!" she laughed.

"Don't you need the tablecloth for Sunday lunch?" I asked.

"I was joking," said Mum. "Go as a vampire. I'll ask Nanny if you can borrow her false teeth!"

"Won't Nanny need her teeth for Sunday lunch?" I asked.

"I was joking again," sighed Mum.

That's the **trouble with jokes** — they're only jokes if they're funny.

"I know, go as the witch from *Snow White*," she said. "You can borrow an apple out of the fruit bowl."

"We've only got bananas in the fruit bowl," I said.

"What about going as Snow Gorilla then?" laughed Mum. "Gorillas love bananas. You can borrow the whole bunch, if you like."

"I'll sort my own costume out, thank you," I told her, going back to my bedroom to think of ideas.

The **trouble with ideas for Halloween costumes** is they are really hard to think of. Especially if you know you might turn into the actual Halloween person you are pretending to be.

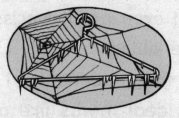

There was no way I wanted to

turn into a werewolf or a witch or even a poultrygeist – which is just as well actually, because there's no wolf hair or black pointy hats in my house to make costumes out of. There isn't even a frog or a newt.

After about an hour I was starting to think I would HAVE to go as a ghost, because ghost costumes were the only ones I knew how to make. I even got the scissors out and everything!

But then, suddenly, I had a genius idea! It was like a wizard had tapped me on the shoulder with a magic wand and given me just the costume idea I had been searching for. All I had to do next was make it.

"MUUUUUM!" I shouted. "PLEASE WILL YOU GO UP IN THE LOFT!"

"WHAT DO YOU WANT ME TO GO UP IN THE LOFT FOR?" my mum shouted back.

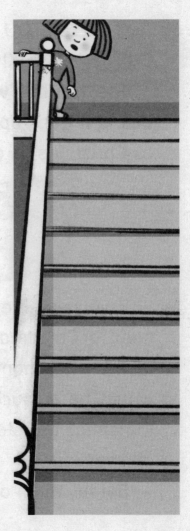

"I NEED YOU TO LOOK IN THE CHRISTMAS BOX!" I explained.

The **trouble with our Christmas box** is it goes up in the loft as soon as Christmas as over.

If you ask me, all the things you need for Christmas are just as exciting all the other months of the year, so it would be a much better idea if the Christmas box stayed in my bedroom all year round.

But my mum always says no.

"What do you want out of the Christmas box?" she asked, not shouting any more because she was at the bottom of the stairs.

"I need a cracker for my Halloween costume," I said. "Can you see if there are any crackers left over from Christmas, please?"

The **trouble with crackers left over from Christmas** is they are exactly the sort of thing children should be allowed to pull all the other months of the year. But my mum always says no to that too.

"If they are good enough to pull this Christmas, they will be good enough to pull next Christmas," she always says. "You are not pulling them for the sake of pulling them. They are going up in the loft."

The **trouble with going up in lofts** is that lofts are really creepy. Even the creak of the loft ladder is creepy.

I've never actually been right up the ladder and into our loft. I've stood on the top step and looked in with a torch, but I've never actually dared to go inside. There is no way I would go up into an actual loft on actual Halloween night day or night night! There could be all sorts of creepy loft monsters hiding up there.

"HOW MANY DO YOU WANT?" my mum shouted down through the hatch.

"HOW MANY CAN I HAVE?" I shouted back.

"HOW MANY DO YOU NEED?" she shouted back.

"ONE," I shouted.

"Then you can have one," she said.

The costume I'd thought of making was perfect, because if it was midnight and there was a full moon, I would be able to change out of it really fast!

"Do you need any help making something to wear?" asked Mum.

"You can help me pull," I said, holding out the cracker and then getting quite excited. I'd never pulled a Christmas cracker in October before!

SNAP! it went.

"BRILLIANT!" I went.

I had everything I needed. All I had to do now was make my costume and get changed.

When I came down from my bedroom just before four o'clock, I decided to creep down the stairs and give my mum the biggest shock of her life.

"*RAH!*" I shouted, jumping into the

kitchen and taking her completely by surprise.

When my mum turned round and saw me, I'm not sure she knew what to say.

For quite a long time actually, she didn't seem to know what to say.

"OK, Daisy, I give up," she said. "Which Halloween horror are you meant to be?"

"I'm Fernando before he turned into the hooley-hooley man, of course!" I told her.

"Of course you are!"
said my mum.

CHAPTER 13

Once I'd got used to being dressed up in a Halloween costume, I actually started to feel OK about going to see Mrs Pike. I mean, I looked really good, in an emergency I could get changed really quickly, and who knows, doing Halloween things with Mrs Pike might not be so bad after all.

Trouble is, when I opened my front door at four o'clock and looked out into the street . . . it wasn't just getting dark, it was getting foggy too.

Really, really, REALLY foggy!

The **trouble with fog** is it makes everything look really ghostly.

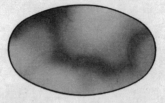

"Do you want me to come with you to knock on Mrs Pike's door?" asked Mum.

"Yes please," I gulped.

The **trouble with stepping out of your house into a front garden that's filling up with Halloween fog** is it feels like ghosts are creeping all around you and touching your face with cold wispy fingers.

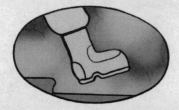

Things got even creepier when we got to Mrs Pike's garden gate, because do you know what was lined up along her drive all the way to her front door? You'll never believe it. Not one scary pumpkin but TEN! With lit up candles inside them too.

I couldn't tell if the pumpkins were haunted ones or not, but you should have seen their teeth! They were like sharks!

"Where do you think Mrs Pike is going to take me in the car?" I asked.

"She's asked me not to tell you," said Mum, "but I promise you it will be fun."

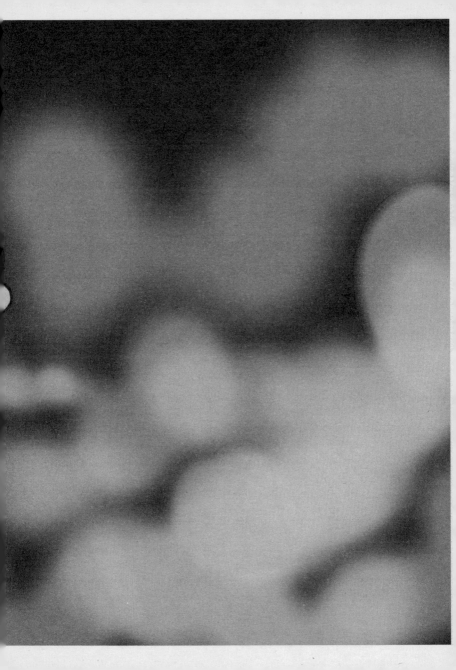

By the time we got to Mrs Pike's front doorstep, all I wanted to do was go home. Because do you know what was dangling from the door-knocker? A great big HAIRY SPIDER! There was no way I was going to knock on a door-knocker like that.

Trouble is, my mum did the knocking instead.

When the front door opened and Mrs Pike looked down at me, I nearly wet myself. I wasn't even sure I was looking at Mrs Pike! Because instead of wearing Mrs Pike-type clothes, the person in front of me had a long red dress on, a black silky cape, green pointy shoes, and hair that didn't look like Mrs Pike hair at all! And you should have seen her face! It wasn't Mrs Pike colour in the slightest. It was whiter than the fog! Well, most of it was. Her eyes were PURPLE! And her chin had been dribbled on with RED BLOOD!

"Didn't you know Mrs Pike was a vampire, Daisy?" Mum smiled. "Have a lovely time together, won't you! I'm off to make some trifle!"

When Mum turned round and left me alone on the doorstep with an actual vampire, I COULDN'T BELIEVE IT!

When Mrs Pike said, "Welcome to my house of horror, Daisy," I nearly

fainted, because do you know what else I saw when she smiled?

WHITE, POINTY VAMPIRE TEETH!

The **trouble with fainting** is it makes it really easy for a vampire to suck all your blood out because you can't put up a struggle. So I had to not faint and go into her house instead.

Mrs Pike's hallway was the creepiest hallway I'd ever seen. There were cobwebs all over the walls, there were more gnashing pumpkins going up the stairs, there were more giant spiders hanging from a lampshade, there was even a

right-way-up bat dangling from the handle of the kitchen door!

"Would you like some fizzy blood, Daisy?" said Mrs Pike. "It tastes just like cherryade."

The **trouble with fizzy blood** is I had never drunk fizzy blood before. It wasn't the fizzy I didn't fancy – it was the blood.

When I asked Mrs Pike if she had orange squash instead, she told me to follow her into the kitchen. So I did. Because I had to. Because if a vampire tells you to do something, you have to do it. Or she might bite you.

"I don't have any orange squash, Daisy," said Mrs Pike, taking a plastic bottle out of her cupboard. "But I do have this." She smiled. "It looks and tastes like orange squash, but actually it's goblin juice."

I'm telling you, if I could have turned myself into a vampire bat and flown straight out of the kitchen window, I definitely would have. But I couldn't. So I didn't. And anyway, the kitchen window was closed.

"There you are, Daisy," said Mrs Pike, pouring me a glass of goblin juice and herself a glass of fizzy blood. "Thank you so much for coming to see me this afternoon.

And may I just say a very happy Halloween to us both!"

CHAPTER 14

Once I was absolutely sure Mrs Pike wasn't going to suck all my blood out, I started to relax. In fact I even tried the fizzy blood too. And guess what? It tasted EXACTLY like cherryade!

Mrs Pike said she always had fizzy blood to drink on Halloween night when she was my age. The fizziest thing I had ever had on Halloween night before was milk!

"Do you think I could do a pumpkin?" I asked. "I've never done a pumpkin before."

"Of course you can, Daisy," said Mrs Pike. "I just need to fetch it in from the garden."

When Mrs Pike came back in, she was carrying the biggest pumpkin I had ever seen.

"I saved the best one for you!" she said, lowering it down onto

the kitchen table.

The **trouble with lowering a pumpkin down onto a kitchen table** is it makes you realize how big a pumpkin can be.

The pumpkin Mrs Pike had given me to carve was GINORMOUS! But the goo inside it was EVEN BETTER!

The **trouble with goo** is I'm not allowed to have goo at home. In case I get too gooey.

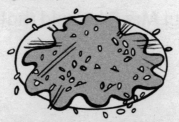

But once we'd cut a star shape in the top of the pumpkin and lifted it off, Mrs Pike let me put my hand right inside!

The goo inside a pumpkin is IMMENSE! Because not only is it all squidgy and cold, it is full of millions and millions of slimy seeds! The more I sloshed my hand around, the more the goo and the slime and the seeds slithered and slimed around my fingers.

To be honest, I'd have been quite happy just squishing and squashing and squidging goo around with my hands, but Mrs Pike said that we had

to get all the goo out of the pumpkin before we could start doing the carving.

The **trouble with getting pumpkin goo out** is it doesn't all come out at once. Some of it you can scoop out with your hands. The rest of it you have to scrape out with a big spoon, because the edges of the inside of a pumpkin are a bit stringy.

Because it was such a big pumpkin, we decided I would get all the goo I could out with my hands, and Mrs Pike

would do the rest with the spoon. You should have seen how full our goo bowl was when we'd finished!

After we'd rinsed and dried our hands, Mrs Pike said we were ready to start carving.

The **trouble with carving** is, if you haven't done it before, then it's best if you let a vampire show you how first.

Especially if you're using a pumpkin carver that is really sharp.

Mrs Pike's pumpkin carver was the business. It had an orange plastic handle and a really thin crinkly blade.

"OK, Daisy," she said, "the first thing we need to do is decide which side of the pumpkin we want the face to be, and then we need to cut out the first eye."

Cutting out pumpkin eyes is really tricky. First you have to work out where the very top of the first eye is going to be, then you have to push the crinkly bit of the carver right through the pumpkin skin in exactly the right spot.

"Now we start carving," said Mrs Pike, using the pumpkin carver like a saw to cut out a triangle shape.

Mrs Pike was an expert. Her triangle shape was brilliant – not too big and not too small – plus, when she pressed it out with her thumb, the hole that was left behind looked exactly like a scary pumpkin eye!

"Right, Daisy," she said, handing me the pumpkin carver. "Your turn."

When I held the pumpkin carver for the first time, I felt a bit nervous. But guess what? I was an expert too!

"FINISHED!" I said, once I'd done all of the face and everything.

"Daisy, that's brilliant!" said Mrs Pike. "That's absolutely amazing . . . only, where are the teeth?"

"I don't want him to have teeth," I told her. "I just want him to have eyes and a nose."

"But why don't you want him to have a mouth?" asked Mrs Pike.

"You don't want to know," I said.

After we'd cleared all the pumpkin things away and had another drink of fizzy blood, Mrs Pike took the lid off the pumpkin I'd carved, put a candle inside and lit it. You should have seen how orange and flickery the eyes and nose looked then – it was brilliant!

It looked even better with the kitchen lights off!

"Would you like me to tell you some scary stories, Daisy?" Mrs Pike asked.

"No, thank you," I said.

"Would you like me to put some make-up on you and turn you into a vampire, just like me?" she asked.

"No, thank you," I said.

"Would you like me to—"

"No, thank you," I said. "Can we just have some more fizzy blood and then maybe talk about nice things instead?"

"Right you are," said Mrs Pike. "I'll open another bottle."

Once we'd drunk another bottle

of fizzy blood and I'd finished telling
Mrs Pike ALLLLLLLL about me, we
suddenly realized how late it was.

"Goodness me," Mrs Pike said, looking at her watch. "Is that the time already?"

"What time is it?" I asked, poking my tongue out to try and see if my tongue had gone red.

"IT'S TRICK-OR-TREATING TIME!" she said, clapping her hands.

CHAPTER 15

The **trouble with trick-or-treating time** is I had never gone trick-or-treating before, so I didn't really know what kind of time I was going to have.

I'd always kind of secretly wanted to try trick-or-treating, but only in the road I live in. Because then I'd be close to my mum if I had to run home. Trouble is, Mrs Pike wanted to go trick-or-treating somewhere else!

"If I tell you the road we are going to, Daisy, it will spoil the surprise," she said, blowing out the candle in my pumpkin and then getting ready to leave the house.

"Make sure you wrap up warm," she said, before blowing out all the candles in the pumpkins on the stairs.

"I will," I said, following her to the door and getting my coat from the coat hook.

"Make sure you do up all the buttons," she said, before picking up a black bin bag.

"I will," I said, tucking my jumper into my trousers first to make me extra safe.

"OK then," said Mrs Pike, opening the front door. "Let's DO THIS!"

The **trouble with opening a front door and doing this** is, when I looked outside, I didn't feel like doing this at all. Because it wasn't Halloween night afternoon any more, it was actual HALLOWEEN NIGHT NIGHT!

Plus, it was REALLY foggy too!

189

"Isn't it exciting, Daisy!" said Mrs Pike, jingling her car keys above her head. "Isn't it atmospheric! I'm going to have to turn on my fog lights!"

The **trouble with fog lights** is I wasn't sure what fog lights were.

But as soon as Mrs Pike switched them on I found out. They made Halloween night fog look even ghostlier! And they showed you how hard fog is to see through.

The **trouble with not being able to see through fog** is, when I looked up at the sky, there was absolutely no way I could see if there was a full moon or not.

When we drove past my front gate, I could barely see my house!

"LOOK, DAISY! Trick-or-treaters!" said Mrs Pike when we got to the top of my road.

It was Roco and Trixie, the children who live at number 7. They were trick-or-treating with their mum.

"LOOK, DAISY! More trick-or-treaters!" she said as we turned slowly into the next road and drove all the way to the end.

The more roads we drove along, the more trick-or-treaters we saw. Some of them I even recognized from school. We didn't just see trick-or-treaters either. We saw some really weird things too.

"Look! There's Christopher Leek!" said Mrs Pike.

"Who's Christopher Leek?" I asked.

"Oh, he's a vampire vegetable," she said. "His brother is Count Dracula."

"Are you really a real actual vampire?" I asked Mrs Pike when we stopped at the first set of traffic lights.

"Goodness no, Daisy," she laughed. "There's no such thing as real vampires – didn't your mum tell you? I'm just pretending to be a vampire for Halloween!!"

"I'm just pretending to be Fernando, the boy who played hide-and-seek with ghosts and ended up as a skeleton covered in cobwebs," I told her.

"Ah, of course!" said Mrs Pike. "I thought that was who you had come as!"

"I made my costume myself," I told her. "Apart from Mum helping me pull the cracker, I did absolutely everything by myself."

"You look fabulous," said Mrs Pike. "Absolutely fabulous."

It was so foggy when Mrs Pike finally parked the car, I had no idea where we were at all. Even if the street lights had been fog lights, I wouldn't have been able to see where we were.

"Welcome, Daisy," Mrs Pike said, undoing her seat belt and then grabbing the black bin bag from the back seat. Welcome, my dear, to . . .

...CHURCH ROAD!"

CHAPTER 16

The **trouble with Church Road** is I'd never been to Church Road before. Not even in the day. So I had no idea what it was like. All I could see was fog.

"Church Road is a wonderful road for trick-or-treating in, Daisy," said Mrs Pike. "I used to come trick-or-treating here when I was a girl. Now, here's a torch for you to shine, and here's a can of silly string for you to squirt. Are you ready to get started, Daisy?"

"I guess so," I said.

"Then let's start at number one!" she said.

It was a good job Mrs Pike had given me a torch, because it helped us find the gate to the first house.

"Now then, Daisy," said Mrs Pike. "This is what we'll do. We'll knock on the front door of every house in the road, and if they open it, we'll shout 'TRICK OR TREAT?' If the person who opens the door says 'TREAT!' they'll give you a treat, like a sweet or some fruit.

"If the person who opens the door says 'TRICK!' then you must squirt them with your silly string and then RUN!"

When I found out that trick-or-treating meant I got to squirt people with silly string and then run, I started to feel much less nervous straight away. I love squirting people with silly string! Even people I don't know!

"What if no one comes to the door?" I asked.

"We go to the next house," said Mrs Pike.

"What do I do if people give me

treats?" I asked.

"You put them in this black bin bag," she said.

"Good, because there is no way I'm going to eat them," I told her.

Walking through the fog to my first ever trick-or-treating door felt really weird. Especially with a grown-up dressed as a vampire behind me.

"I'll ring the doorbell!" said Mrs Pike, leaning over me and pressing it with one of her long purple fingernails. "You get ready to say 'Trick or treat?'"

As soon as the doorbell rang, I put my hand inside my coat pocket.

As soon as the door opened, I got ready to squirt my silly string.

"TRICK OR TREAT?!" shouted Mrs Pike, before I'd even had a chance to say or do anything.

"Treat!" said the lady, holding out a big box of sweets.

The **trouble with ladies saying "Treat!"** is it means you're not allowed to squirt them with silly string.

You have to take a sweet out of the box instead.

"Take two, take three!" said the lady.

Did she think I was MAD?

"Thank you so much!" said Mrs Pike, holding the bag out for me to drop my poisoned sweet into and then waving goodbye to the lady. "HAPPY HALLOWEEN!

"What a good start!" she said as we headed back down the path in the direction of house number two.

Good start? It was a rubbish start, if you ask me. All I wanted to do was squirt someone with silly string.

The **trouble with wanting to squirt someone with silly string** is if everyone who opens their door says "TREAT!" then there is no way you can do it.

And guess what? The lady at number 2 Church Road said "TREAT!", the man at number 3 Church Road said "TREAT!", the children at number 4 said "TREAT!" and the lady at number 5 said "TREAT!" The people at numbers 6 and 9 didn't say "TREAT!", but that was only because they didn't answer the door. Everyone else all the way up to house number 12 kept on saying "TREAT!"

It was SO UNFAIR!

"If someone doesn't answer, can I squirt their door instead?" I asked Mrs Pike.

"OOOH no, Daisy," she said. "You

214

don't want to waste your silly string on a silly old front door, you want to squirt it all over someone! Let's keep going. Our bag is really filling up, you know! Perhaps the people at number thirteen will say 'TRICK!' Let's go and see!"

So we went and saw.

And just my luck, it was just

"TREAT!

TREAT!

TREAT!"

all the way!

By the time we got to the middle
of Church Road, I'd been given a
poisoned toffee,
   a poisoned packet
of Refreshers,

three poisoned
   lollipops,
two poisoned
apples,

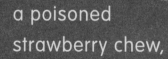

a poisoned
strawberry chew,

216

a poisoned banana
flump, a packet of
poisoned crisps,
four poisoned mints,
a packet of poisoned
chewing gum and a
poisoned "sugar rat" that wasn't a

sugar rat at all, it was a sugar mouse.
Because I've seen sugar mice before.
And anyway sugar rats would be far
too scary to eat. w

By the time we got to the end of the road I had lost count of how many poisonous things we had in the bag. All I knew was, I hadn't got to squirt anyone with my silly string! Not even a teensy squirt. Or even a weensy squirt! Because everyone in Church Road only knows how to say "TREAT!"

And NOT "TRICK!"!!!!!

It was soooooo ANNOYING!

"Wasn't that wonderful!" said Mrs Pike, shining her torch back down the path of number 32. "Wasn't that FUN! I told you it would be fun, didn't I, Daisy? But I'm afraid this is the end of Church Road."

The **trouble with the end of Church Road** is it meant there would be no more chances to squirt my silly string.

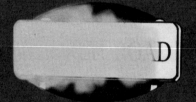

"Can't we go back the other way and do the houses on the other side of the road too?" I asked.

"There are no houses on the other side of Church Road, Daisy," said Mrs Pike, flashing her torch through the fog. "All you'll see is fields."

When Mrs Pike said there were

fields on the other side of Church Road, I didn't believe her at first. I'd never heard of roads that didn't have houses on both sides, but when I pointed my torch in the same direction as hers, I saw that it was true. There were no gates, no walls, no houses, no front doors – there weren't even any street lamps on the other side of Church Road.

All there was was fog!

"Number 32 is the very last building in the road, Daisy," said Mrs Pike, flashing her torch through the fog. "Unless you include the church."

The **trouble** **with** **including** **churches** is trick-or-treaters should never include churches. Especially churches in the dark in the fog in the countryside on Halloween night. Anyone knows that.

Except Mrs Pike.

"Wait a moment! You've given me an idea, Daisy!" she suddenly said, putting her arm round me and leading me towards a creepy, creaky, cobwebby wooden gate.

"Let's include the church! You'll LOVE the church at the end of Church Road, Daisy – especially the church at the end of Church Road ON HALLOWEEN!"

"Will I be able to squirt the vicar with silly string?" I asked, squeezing through the gate.

"I'm not sure the vicar will be in the church at this time of night," Mrs Pike whispered. "But I'll tell you what you can do," she said, shining her torch under her chin and making her face look super creepy. "Are you feeling brave, Daisy?"

"Not really," I said.

"Are you feeling really, REALLY brave, Daisy?" she whispered.

"I don't think so," I said. But she still wasn't listening.

"You can play MURDER IN THE GRAVEYARD with me!" she cackled.

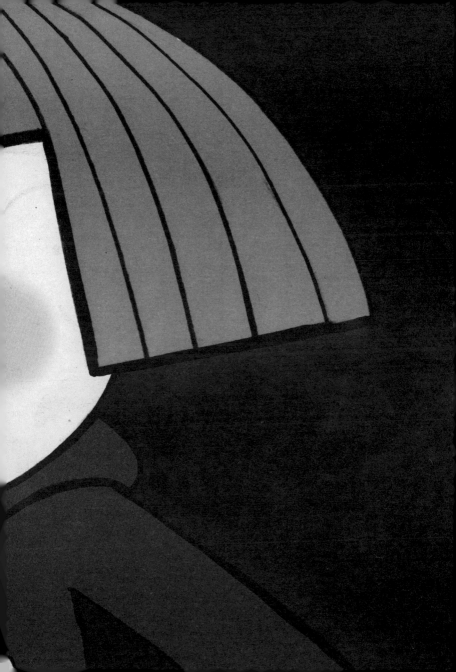

CHAPTER 17

The **trouble with grown-ups who don't have any children** is there is no way they should be allowed anywhere near other people's children. Especially on Halloween night!

Was I feeling brave? NO, I WAS NOT! Did I want to play Murder in the Graveyard? No, I DID NOT! I mean, what kind of grown-up takes a child anywhere near a GRAVEYARD in the DARK in the FOG in the COUNTRYSIDE on HALLOWEEN NIGHT, and then says, "Let's play MURDER IN THE GRAVEYARD!!!"?

Trouble is, before I could even say anything, Mrs Pike was already telling me the rules!

"Now then, Daisy," she said, "close your eyes and start counting while I go and find a gravestone to hide behind. As soon as you've counted to a hundred, shout, 'I'm coming to murder you, ready or not!' and then use your torch to come and find me. As soon as you find the gravestone

I'm hiding behind, you can murder me with your silly string!"

I couldn't believe my ears. Not only had Mrs Pike taken me to a graveyard in the dark in the fog in the countryside on Halloween night – now she was going to run off and leave me all ALONE, with only a torch and some silly string to defend myself with!

There was no way I was closing my eyes. What if an owl or a werewolf or a zombie or a witch or a vampire tried to get me while she was hiding?

What if the hooley-hooley man came along looking for a new wardrobe?

It's a good job I didn't close my eyes too. Because if I hadn't kept my torch on and my eyes open while Mrs Pike was running away from me, I would never have seen her disappear.

Yes, DISAPPEAR.

Completely out of sight.

Just like that!

In the dark.

In the fog.

RIGHT BEFORE MY VERY EYES!

It was like a magic trick. One second she was there. The next second she was GONE!

But where had she gone?

And how had she gone?

Was she actually a vampire after all?

And if she was, had she turned into a bat and flown away?

And if she had turned into a bat and flown away, was she flying in my direction LOOKING FOR BLOOD?

I was so shocked, I couldn't move, I couldn't think, I could barely even remember my own name!

At least, I couldn't until a voice in the foggy darkness shouted, "DAISY!"

It was the voice of Mrs Pike.

"DAISY!" she shouted again. "I've fallen down a hole! Come and help me!"

CHAPTER 18

The **trouble with someone playing Murder in the Graveyard and then falling down a hole** is, Mrs Pike had fallen down a whopper.

In fact, the hole she had fallen into was so deep, I couldn't even see the top of her head. At least I couldn't until I shone my torch down on to her face.

"Daisy you need to help me!" Mrs Pike said, reaching up with her arm. "It's all muddy and cold and wet down here. Please try and pull me out!"

The **trouble with trying to pull a grown-up out of a deep hole** is you need to be much bigger than me to be able to do it.

AAAAAARGHHHHH!

"We need to phone for help, Daisy,"
said Mrs Pike. "Can you go back to
my car? If I give you my car keys, do
you think you could go and fetch my
phone? It's in my handbag."

Was she serious!?

Not only was I standing in a
graveyard in the dark in the fog
staring at a vampire down a hole, now
I was going to have to walk through
a graveyard, past a church, through
a gate, past thirty-two houses, right
to the very end of Church Road in
the dark in the fog in the countryside
ON HALLOWEEN NIGHT ALL ON MY
OWN!!!!

And then ALL THE WAY BACK AGAIN!

"On second thoughts, Daisy," she said, "you'd better stay here with me. Your mum would never forgive me if I lost you."

As soon as Mrs Pike changed her mind, I was totally sure she wasn't a real vampire. A real vampire would definitely have made a child get their mobile from a car. Plus, thinking about it, a real vampire would have turned into a bat and flown out of the hole.

Mrs Pike definitely couldn't fly. All she could do was jump and scrabble and slip and slide and scrabble and fall over in the mud.

"Do you want me to go and knock on the door of number 32 again?" I asked, really, really hoping she would say no.

"No, Daisy. I'm not letting you out of my sight for another minute," she said. "We'll just have to wait till someone comes along."

The **trouble with waiting for someone to come along** is not many people come along in a graveyard in the dark in the fog in the countryside on Halloween night.

"Who do you think might come along?" I asked.

"The vicar, hopefully," she said. "Or a choir."

"Not a zombie?" I said.

"No, not a zombie, Daisy," she said. "There are no such things as zombies."

"Not a vampire?" I said.

"No, not a vampire, Daisy," she said. "I've told you before, there are no such things as vampires."

"Not a ghost or a witch or a poultrygeist or the hooley-hooley man?" I said, flashing my torch down onto her face and expecting her to say no to those too.

. . .

. . .

. . .

. . .

Except she didn't.

She didn't speak.

She didn't blink.

All she did was point into the fog with her torch.

"What's wrong?" I said, starting to get a bit nervous and then jumping out of my skin when her lips suddenly started working.

"Behind you, Daisy!" Mrs Pike trembled. "BEHIND YOU!"

Honestly, I have never spun round so fast in my life. When I saw what was behind me, I nearly died on the spot.

It was a skeleton! And it was staring straight at me!

Quick as a flash, I grabbed my silly string and fired!

SQUIRT!

SQUIRT!!

SQUIRT!!!

SQUIRT!!!!

SQUIIIIIRT!!!!

CHAPTER 19

It was only when I'd run out that I realized it was a skeleton on a bike.

"Hello, Daisy," said Jack Beechwhistle, wiping the string off his face. "What's she doing down that hole?"

When I heard Jack Beechwhistle's voice coming out of the skeleton's face, I was so relieved. I'd never been so pleased to see him in my life.

"She's trying to get out," I said. "Sorry for squirting you. Her name is Mrs Pike. She's my neighbour. We were playing Murder in the Graveyard."

When Jack found out I'd been playing Murder in the Graveyard, he was really impressed. Especially Murder in the Graveyard in the dark in the fog in the countryside on Halloween night.

"I come here on my bike every Halloween night," he said, "to see if there are any zombies that need teaching a lesson."

"Me too," I fibbed.

"Do you like my skeleton hoodie?" he asked. "It's got trousers too," he said, pointing at the bones on his legs.

"Yes, they're really good," I fibbed again.

"So why doesn't she climb out?" asked Jack, walking to the edge of the hole and looking down.

"She's tried to, but she keeps slipping on the mud," I whispered.

"I bet I could climb my way out of there," he said. "I could climb my way out of any hole, however deep, because I've got escape skills. And by the way, it's not a hole, it's a grave. Someone is going to be buried there next week."

When I realized that Mrs Pike was trapped inside a hole that wasn't a hole but a GRAVE, I shivered from top to toe.

"What if no one can get her out?" I gasped.

"Then she'll have to be buried alongside the coffin," Jack whispered.

I wasn't sure if Mrs Pike knew she was in a grave or not, or if she could hear what we were saying. But when she started waving and flashing her torch beam across our

faces, I knew she wanted us to get her out fast.

"Do you think we could both lift her out?" I asked Jack.

"Normally, I'd lift her out on my own," he whispered, "but I sprained my shoulder this morning doing black-belt jujitsu training with Colin and Harry."

Which might have been a fib. I wasn't sure.

"Why hasn't she rung for help on her mobile?" asked Jack.

"Her phone is in the car," I whispered.

"Where's her car?" whispered Jack.

"At the beginning of Church Road," I told him.

"Who was she going to ring?" asked Jack.

"My mum," I told him.

"I'll go and get her!" he said.

CHAPTER 20

"Where do you live?" Jack asked, speeding back up the church path again.

"Fourteen Bilberry Way," I told him.

"I'll be as quick as I can!" he promised.

CHAPTER 21

It was about half an hour before my mum finally came to rescue Mrs Pike. When she appeared out of the fog, I thought she was a ghost, her face looked so white. But ghosts don't carry stepladders. At least, I don't think they do.

My mum had been really worried about us. Apparently she had been ringing and ringing and ringing Mrs Pike to find out where we were.

It was a really good idea to bring a stepladder, because Mrs Pike's hands were so muddy and wet, my mum would never have been able to get hold of her.

When Mrs Pike finally crawled out of the hole, she looked more like a mud monster than a vampire. She even groaned like a mud monster when she stood up.

I could barely see the church clock through the fog, but when my mum put her arm around Mrs Pike and told her everything was going to be all right, I knew it was time to go home.

We were at the end of the church path when Jack caught up with us on his bike. I think he'd had to cycle quite a long way to get my mum.

"Do you fancy going trick-or-treating?" he asked me as we squeezed through the gate. "It's only nine o'clock."

"I've already been trick-or-treating," I told him. "And anyway, I thought you said you only did trick-or-tricking?"

"I do," he said. "I was tricking you."

When I showed Jack the bag of sweets me and Mrs Pike had collected, he said they were some of the most poisonous he'd ever seen. So I gave them to him straight away.

"It's a good job you didn't eat any of them," he said. "If you had, you

would probably have been dead by now, or at the very least your face would have turned purple and yellow and your tongue would have dropped off."

"Thanks for taking them," I said.

"See you at school on Monday," Jack said, standing up on his pedals and then cycling away into the fog.

CHAPTER 22

When me and mum arrived home, Mrs Pike's pumpkins weren't on her driveway any more. They were in the bin.

"I don't think she meant to fall down the hole," I said, as Mum opened the front door and let us into the house. "It was so dark and foggy in the graveyard, she couldn't see where she was going."

"What you were doing playing hide-and-seek games in a graveyard, I really do not know," said Mum. "I thought you were going trick-or-treating not potholing."

"It wasn't my idea," I told her. "It was totally Mrs Pike's idea, not mine."

"It doesn't matter whose idea it was." Mum frowned. "It was a bad idea with a capital B."

As soon as I'd taken off my coat, I had a brilliant idea with a capital M.

"Can we play murder in the dark?!" I asked. "PLEASE, PLEASE, PLEASE! Just you and me, no churches, no graveyards, no gravestones or graves to fall into either, just normal murder in the dark in the house!"

"No, Daisy, we cannot," said Mum. "The only game you are going to play now is getting ready for bed with a capital GRFB."

"But tonight is Halloween night!" I moaned.

"Not in our house, it isn't," she growled.

The **trouble with it not being Halloween night in our house** is it blooming well felt like it was Halloween night in our house.

Especially after going to a graveyard with a vampire. Double especially after putting my pyjamas on. And triple especially after having to walk up the stairs to my bedroom on my own.

If only I hadn't peeped through my bedroom curtains to see if there were any vampires outside.

The **trouble with peeping through my bedroom curtains** is that's when I noticed there was a fullish moon.

YES, A FULLISH MOON, peeping through the fog!

Not only that, it was looking STRAIGHT AT ME!

There was no way I could get to sleep knowing there was a fullish moon staring at my curtains!

When I heard my mum going to bed later, I couldn't even begin to close my eyes, I was so nervous.

I mean, if there was a fullish moon at a quarter past ten, there could be an even fuller moon by twelve o'clock midnight! Especially on Halloween!!!!!!

What if Mum was turning into a witch?

What if the zombies were already gunging through the floor of my classroom?

What if a haunted headmaster was floating across the playground?

What if the hooley-hooley man had decided to move into my new wardrobe?

What if vampire bats were

heading for my letter box?

What if haunted tea towels were coming out of my mum's laundry basket?

What if Mrs Pike's haunted pumpkins were coming to bite me?

What if werewolves could sniff the meat for our Sunday lunch?

If there was a fullish moon and it was midnight and it was Halloween, ANYTHING could happen!

It was 11.04.

My mum was asleep.

The house was all dark.

I had Mrs Pike's torch and fifty-six minutes to totally build my defences!

CHAPTER 23

The **trouble with building Halloween defences** is you can never be totally sure you've done enough.

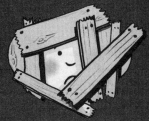

It was twenty-seven seconds to midnight when I finally dived under my bedcovers last night, and quarter past nine when I finally plucked up the courage to pull back my covers and peep out again this morning!

The first thing I noticed was I was still alive. I still had all my blood in me, which meant a vampire hadn't got me. I wasn't covered in cobwebs, which meant I hadn't turned into Fernando. I hadn't been got by a zombie or a werewolf or a ghost. WHICH MEANT MY HALLOWEEN DEFENCES HAD TOTALLY WORKED!!!

If only I'd had time to tidy up before my mum woke up too . . .

"Morning, Daisy," she said, stopping to wave to me on her way to the loo and then rubbing her eyes.

. . .

"OH NO, DAISY, YOU HAVEN'T . . ." she said, looking in the toilet.

"OH NO, DAISY, YOU HAVEN'T . . ." she said, looking into my bedroom.

"OH NO, DAISY, YOU HAVEN'T . . ." she said, looking down the stairs.

"OH NO, DAISY, YOU HAVEN'T . . ." she said, going downstairs and into the kitchen.

Trouble is, I had.

The **trouble with thinking my mum is turning into a witch** is I had to put all of her undercover wands down the toilet.

no entry

The **trouble with defending myself against vampires** is I didn't have any garlics, so I had to use gravy granules instead.

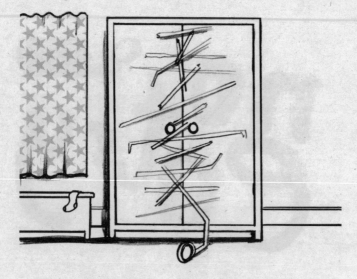

The **trouble with defending my wardrobe against the hooley-hooley man** is hammer and nails would have been too noisy, so I had to use sellotape instead.

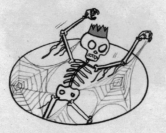

The **trouble with needing a feather duster made of golden dodo feathers** is I had to use golden syrup instead.

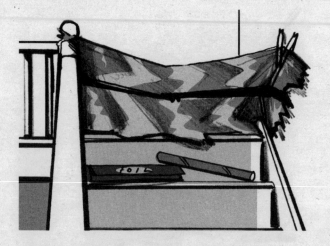

The **trouble with defending myself against werewolves** is I didn't have any silver bullets, so I had to put silver foil on the stairs instead.

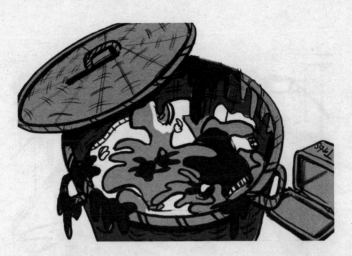

The **trouble with defending myself against haunted tea towels** is I didn't have the right colour pegs, so I gunged them with my mum's Liquitabs instead.

The **trouble with fighting gunge with gunge** is I couldn't find any gunge, so I had to use trifle instead.

My mum didn't sound very happy.

"DAISY!!!!!!"

She definitely didn't sound very happy.

"MY BEST TABLECLOTH!"

Especially when she found the tablecloth that I'd nearly had to use for my Halloween costume and came stomping back up the stairs . . .

Uh-oh . . . it's THE MUMMY!!!!!!!!!!

DAISY'S
TROUBLE INDEX

The trouble with . . .

Daisy's Halloween Quiz:

How much can you remember from the story? Test yourself!

1. According to Jack Beechwhistle, where does the water in the school drinking fountain come from?

2. What metal does Jack insist werewolves are allergic to?

3. What does Daisy's mum plan to cook for dinner when Nanny and Grampy come to their house?

4. What item of clothing does Daisy worry a zombie might have tampered with?

5. As well as normal and ugly, what's the third type of ghost?

6. What cooking ingredient does Jack tell Daisy will scare vampires away?

7. What was the hooley-hooley man's real name?

8. What does Daisy ask her mum to fetch from up in the loft, to be part of her Halloween costume?

9. When Daisy carves her pumpkin, what does she decide to leave out?

10. Who does Daisy squirt with her can of silly string?

Spot the Difference

Can you spot the ten differences between these pictures?

Answers

Daisy's Halloween Quiz:

1. The wicked well
2. Silver
3. A roast dinner
4. Ankle socks
5. Headless
6. Garlic
7. Fernando
8. A Christmas cracker
9. The teeth
10. Jack Beechwhistle

Spot the Difference

Have you read these other Daisy adventures?